THE BOOKS

MEET SAMANTHA · An American Girl

Samantha becomes good friends with Nellie, a servant girl, and together they plan a secret midnight adventure.

❧

SAMANTHA LEARNS A LESSON · A School Story

Samantha becomes Nellie's teacher, but Nellie has some very important lessons to teach Samantha, too.

❧

SAMANTHA'S SURPRISE · A Christmas Story

Uncle Gard's friend Cornelia is ruining Samantha's Christmas. But Christmas morning brings surprises!

❧

HAPPY BIRTHDAY, SAMANTHA! · A Springtime Story

When Eddie Ryland spoils Samantha's birthday party, Cornelia's twin sisters know just what to do.

❧

SAMANTHA SAVES THE DAY · A Summer Story

Samantha enjoys a peaceful summer at Piney Point, until a terrible storm strands her on Teardrop Island!

❧

CHANGES FOR SAMANTHA · A Winter Story

When Samantha finds out that her friend Nellie is living in an orphanage, she must think of a way to help her escape.

HAPPY BIRTHDAY, SAMANTHA!

A SPRINGTIME STORY

BY VALERIE TRIPP

ILLUSTRATIONS ROBERT GRACE, N. NILES

VIGNETTES JANA FOTHERGILL

PLEASANT COMPANY

PICTURE CREDITS

The following individuals and organizations have generously given
permission to reprint illustrations contained in "Looking Back":
pp. 58-59—State Historical Society of Wisconsin; State Historical Society
of Wisconsin; Kansas Collection, University of Kansas Libraries; From the
collection of Mrs. Edward Thiele; pp. 60-61—State Historical Society of
Wisconsin; Courtesy *Women Are Here to Stay*, Agnes Rogers, New York:
Harper, 1949; From the Pitman Collection; Courtesy Staten Island
Historical Society; p. 62—Courtesy Library of Congress; State Historical
Society of Wisconsin.

Robert Grace dedicates his illustrations in this book to the memory of his
friend, Kenneth Michael Goddard.

Edited by Jeanne Thieme
Designed by Myland McRevey
Art Directed by Kathleen A. Brown

Library of Congress Cataloging-in-Publication Data

Tripp, Valerie, 1951-
Happy birthday, Samantha!: a springtime story

(The American girls collection)
Summary: A ten-year-old girl discovers the modern delights of turn-of-
the-century New York City when she travels there with her
grandmother to visit relatives.
[1. New York (N.Y.)—Fiction]
I. Grace, R. (Robert), ill.   II. Niles, Nancy, ill.   III. Title.   IV. Series.
PZ7.T7363Har 1987   [Fic]   87-14074
ISBN 0-937295-89-2
ISBN 0-937295-35-3 (pbk.)

TO
CHRISTOPHER WALLACE DRAPER

TABLE OF CONTENTS

SAMANTHA'S FAMILY

GRANDMARY
*Samantha's
grandmother, who
wants her
to be a young lady.*

AGNES & AGATHA
*Samantha's newest
friends, who are
Cornelia's sisters.*

SAMANTHA
*An orphan who lives
with her wealthy
grandmother.*

UNCLE GARD
*Samantha's
favorite uncle, who
calls her Sam.*

AUNT CORNELIA
*An old-fashioned
beauty who has
new-fangled ideas.*

HAWKINS

*Grandmary's butler
and driver, who
is Samantha's friend.*

MRS. HAWKINS

*The cook, who
always has a treat
for Samantha.*

JESSIE

*Grandmary's
seamstress, who
"patches
Samantha up."*

ELSA

*The maid, who
is usually grumpy.*

EDDIE

*Samantha's
neighbor who loves
to tease.*

PETTICOATS AND PETIT FOURS

"SURPRISE!" shouted two excited voices. "Happy birthday, Samantha!"

Samantha sat up and rubbed her eyes. Two red-headed curlytops whirled into her room, jumped up on her bed, and pushed a huge bouquet of roses into her arms. "This is for you!" said the redhead named Agnes.

"Jiminy!" exclaimed Samantha. "It's beautiful!"

"We made it ourselves," added Agatha proudly. Agatha looked exactly like Agnes. They were Aunt Cornelia's twin sisters. Now that Uncle Gard and Cornelia were married, Agnes and Agatha were Samantha's newest friends and favorite relatives.

Samantha put her nose deep into the roses.

"Thank you!" she said. "No one ever gave me flowers for my birthday before."

"I knew you'd like them," said Agnes happily. "It was my idea to give you a bouquet."

"Well, it was my idea to wrap the stems in lace," insisted Agatha.

Samantha looked at the bottom of the bouquet. "Where did you get all this nice lace?" she asked. "It looks sort of like it came off a petticoat."

The twins looked at each other and giggled.

"Did you cut up your petticoat?" Samantha asked.

"Not exactly," said Agatha. She leaned back and twisted one of her red curls around her finger. "There was already a rip where the ruffle was attached. We just sort of helped the rip get bigger until the ruffle fell off."

"Gosh!" said Samantha. "Grandmary would be furious if I cut up one of my petticoats. Won't your mother be angry?"

"Oh, no," said Agnes lightly. "That petticoat was getting too small for us anyway."

"Besides," said Agatha, "our mother is used to us and our ideas by now."

Samantha laughed out loud. Sometimes it seemed to her that Agnes and Agatha's ideas spilled out all over the place, like popcorn popping out of a pot. During the week of their visit, the twins had turned Grandmary's quiet house in Mount Bedford topsy-turvy. Samantha liked it that way.

Agnes sprawled on Samantha's bed, swinging her legs over the side. "Hurry and get dressed," she said. "We smelled something absolutely scrumptious coming from the kitchen."

"Ooooh! I bet Mrs. Hawkins is making a birthday treat for breakfast!" said Samantha as she scrambled out of bed. "I'll be dressed in a jiffy." She pulled her long underwear out of the drawer.

"Oh, don't bother with that," said Agnes. "No one wears long underwear anymore." Agnes and Agatha were from New York City, so they knew all about the latest fashions.

"I *have* to wear it," sighed Samantha. "It's one of Grandmary's rules: long underwear from September to the end of June." She pulled the itchy underwear onto one leg.

"Jeepers!" exclaimed Agatha. "What an old-

3

"Then don't wear long underwear," said Agnes.
"Make up your own mind for once."

fashioned rule! You'll roast if you wear that today."

Samantha held out her leg and looked at the underwear. "I do hate it," she said.

"Then don't wear it," said Agnes simply. "Make up your own mind for once."

Samantha sat up very straight. "I'm ten years old today," she said. "I guess that's old enough to think for myself about things like underwear." She peeled off the underwear, rolled it up into a ball, and shoved it to the back of the dresser drawer. When she pulled her stockings on over her bare legs, she felt deliciously light and free.

"Come on," she said to the twins as she buttoned up her dress. "Let's go have breakfast." She grabbed her bouquet off the bed. "I can't wait to show these roses to Hawkins."

"Hawkins has already seen them," said Agatha as the girls trotted down the hall. "They're from his bush."

Samantha stopped still. "Uh oh," she said. "No one is allowed to touch Hawkins' special rosebush. No one!"

"Don't worry," laughed Agnes. "There were millions of roses on that bush. Hawkins won't mind that we borrowed a few."

And to Samantha's surprise, Agnes was right. Hawkins didn't mind about the roses. "What a lovely birthday surprise!" he said. His eyes twinkled. "Mrs. Hawkins and I have a birthday surprise for you, too, Miss Samantha." He pushed open the kitchen door and there was Mrs. Hawkins with a plate of blueberry muffins. One of the muffins had a candle stuck right in the middle.

"Oooh!" exclaimed Samantha. "Blueberry muffins!"

"Quick! Make a wish!" said Agatha. "Blow out the candle."

"That's easy," laughed Samantha. She scrunched her eyes shut and wished that being ten would be completely different from being nine. She was ready for some changes. Then she blew the candle out with one puff.

As the twins clapped, Mrs. Hawkins said, "Well, that *was* easy. But this afternoon, you'll have a cake with ten candles. You'll surely have to huff and puff then, love."

Agatha bounced on her chair. "I have a wonderful idea, Mrs. Hawkins!" she exclaimed.

"Instead of one cake with ten candles, you could make ten little cakes and put a candle on each one of them!"

"Ten cakes?" asked Mrs. Hawkins. She sounded doubtful.

"Ten little teeny tiny cakes," said Agatha. "They're called petit fours. Ladies have them at all the fancy tea parties in New York."

"Petit fours," Samantha repeated. "They sound so elegant. Could you try to make them, Mrs. Hawkins? Please?"

"Well, I don't know," said Mrs. Hawkins slowly. "We never had anything so different before."

"That's why it's such a wonderful idea," pleaded Samantha. "No one in Mount Bedford has ever had ten cakes. All the girls will be so surprised."

Mrs. Hawkins smiled at Samantha. "If you want ten cakes you shall have them, love," she said. "I guess I can try something new."

"I have an idea for something new, too," Agnes piped up. "What if you shaped each girl's ice cream in a little ice cream mold? That's how they do it at the big ice cream parlors in the city."

Samantha was very excited. The twins had such good ideas! "Could we change the ice cream, too?" she asked Hawkins. "Except I still want it to be peppermint. That's my absolute favorite kind."

Hawkins laughed. "We can change the shape of the ice cream without changing the flavor," he said. "As soon as I've washed the ice cream freezer, you may help me make it."

"Meanwhile, you chickadees scoot outside," said Mrs. Hawkins, rolling up her sleeves. "I don't want you underfoot while I'm making your petit fours."

Samantha and the twins finished their blueberry muffins and hurried outside into the sunshine. The trees were covered with shiny green leaves as if they'd decorated themselves in honor of Samantha's birthday. Samantha was telling the twins how ice cream was made when a voice behind them said, "Hey, carrot heads."

It was Eddie Ryland, Samantha's pesty next-door neighbor.

Agnes scowled at him. "Don't say 'hey,'" she

said. "Hay is for horses."

"You ought to know," said Eddie. "You eat like a horse."

The girls rolled their eyes at each other while Eddie laughed at his own joke. "So what are you ninnies doing today?" he went on.

"Nothing," said all three girls quickly.

But just at that moment, Hawkins appeared with the freezer.

"I know! You're making ice cream!" said Eddie. "I know *everything* about ice cream. I'll help."

"No!" said the girls in one voice.

"You just go away, Eddie," Agatha ordered.

"Who's going to make me?" Eddie challenged.

"*I'll* make you," Agatha began. Samantha saw that Agatha was making a fist. She knew Agatha would punch Eddie right in the nose if she wanted to. Not even Grandmary's strictest rule—GIRLS DON'T FIGHT—would stop Agatha once she was mad.

"Oh, all right, Eddie," Samantha said quickly. "You can help us make ice cream, but don't be a pest." She whispered to the twins, "Just ignore him. Maybe he'll go away."

The girls and Eddie watched as Hawkins poured ice chips into the ice cream freezer. "Now it's time to add the salt," said Samantha. She scooped up handfuls of rock salt from a sack and poured the salt on the ice.

"Use just enough to keep the ice melted," warned Hawkins.

"And keep it away from the lid of the container," Eddie added in a know-it-all voice. "Because if any salt gets inside, the ice cream will be ruined."

"We don't need you to boss us, Eddie," said

Agatha. She pushed her shoulder in front of Eddie to block his view.

"This ice cream is going to be the best ice cream anyone ever ate," Samantha said happily as Hawkins began turning the crank of the freezer.

"I can't wait to taste it," said Agnes.

"Me, either," said Samantha.

"Me, either," said Agatha.

"Me, either," said Eddie. But the girls just ignored him.

C H A P T E R

T W O

—

THE PARTY

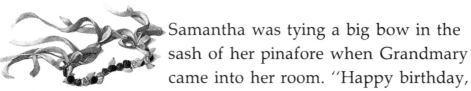

Samantha was tying a big bow in the sash of her pinafore when Grandmary came into her room. "Happy birthday, dear," she said. "I have something special for you to wear at your party. Turn and face the mirror."

Samantha was very still while Grandmary stood behind her and fastened an old-fashioned circlet of silk rosebuds in her hair. "Oh, Grandmary," Samantha sighed. "It's lovely."

Grandmary smiled. "Your mother wore this circlet at her tenth birthday party. I'm sure she would have been happy to see it passed on to you now. You look just as pretty as she did."

"Thank you very much," Samantha said.

"You are welcome, my dear," said Grandmary. "Now let's go down and wait for your guests. It's almost time for them to arrive."

Samantha felt fluttery with excitement as she stood in front of the house next to Grandmary. She couldn't wait until her friends saw the wonderful surprises she and the twins had planned for them. One by one the girls came up the walk, dressed in their very best party dresses. Each girl carried her favorite doll in one arm and a brightly-wrapped present for Samantha in the other. Even though Samantha knew everyone well, she felt a little shy as her friends said hello and curtsied to her and to Grandmary. The guests were shy, too, especially when they saw Agnes and Agatha. The twins looked very grown-up in their pale blue dresses, which were the latest style from New York.

The girls sat quietly in a circle of wicker chairs on the sunny side lawn. They sat up straight, their legs crossed at the ankles. Their dolls sat up straight, too, and stared at each other across the circle. Samantha tried to begin a polite, grown-up conversation. "Well," she said at last. "It certainly is a nice day."

The girls sat up straight, their legs crossed at the ankles.
Their dolls sat up straight, too.

"Yes!" everyone agreed. Then all the girls were quiet again. A breeze ruffled their big hairbows and the skirts of their dresses. It looked as if a flock of pale butterflies was fluttering rather nervously over the smooth green grass.

No one seemed to have anything to say, so Samantha tried again. "It is quite warm though—"

"Why don't you open your gifts?" Agnes interrupted.

"Good idea," murmured the rest of the girls. One by one they stepped forward and handed Samantha their presents. Everyone oohed and ahhed politely as she opened a box of colored pencils from Ida, a fan from Ruth, and a big book of piano exercises from Edith Eddleton. Agnes and Agatha kept their present for the last. They giggled as they came forward together and handed Samantha a big square box.

Samantha lifted the lid and held up a stout, cheerful-looking stuffed bear. Everyone squealed with delight. "A teddy bear!" exclaimed Samantha. "I love it!" She gave the bear a big hug.

"Teddy bears are the newest thing in New York," said Agnes, beaming. "We wanted you to

15

have one of your very own."

"Thanks!" said Samantha.

"Oh, may I hold him?" asked Ida. "He's just so cute."

The friendly bear was passed from girl to girl. But after he had gone around the circle, the party got too quiet again. Everyone was trying so hard to be polite and grown-up, they were as stiff as the lace on their collars.

Samantha was relieved when a car came roaring up the drive with an ear-splitting ooh-wah! ooh-wah! "Uncle Gard! Aunt Cornelia!" she exclaimed. Her guests bounced out of their chairs. "Hello! Hello!" they called as they followed Samantha over to the car.

Uncle Gard came straight to Samantha without even stopping to take off his driving goggles. He lifted her up into the air. "Happy samday, Bertha!" he said. All the girls giggled and Uncle Gard pretended to be confused. "Wait a minute. That's not right," he said. "I'll have to do that over." He lifted Samantha up again, gave her a kiss, and said, "Happy birthday, Samantha!"

"Oh, Gard!" laughed Aunt Cornelia. She leaned

16

over and gave Samantha a soft kiss. "Happy, happy birthday, Samantha," she said. "There's someone I'd like you to meet." Aunt Cornelia reached into the car and lifted out a little brown and white puppy. "This is Jip, the newest member of our family," she explained.

When Samantha took Jip in her arms, he reached up and licked her chin with his warm, rough tongue. "He's perfect," Samantha sighed.

"Put him down," said Agatha, "and I'll make him do his tricks."

"Remember to keep an eye on him," warned Cornelia as Samantha carried Jip over to the side lawn. "He's frisky and he likes to run."

Samantha put Jip on the grass inside the circle of chairs. "Sit, Jip," commanded Agatha. Jip wagged his tail, but he didn't sit. "He doesn't always do what you ask him to," Agatha admitted. "Sit, Jip!" she commanded again. But Jip ignored her. He began to run wildly around the circle of girls, barking at their feet.

"He likes shoes," explained Agnes. So all the girls sat in their chairs and danced their feet up and down in front of Jip. Jip ran from girl to girl, growling and jumping at their shoes and having a wonderful time. Then Agatha's foot knocked over a box, and the teddy bear tumbled out. To the girls' delight, Jip began to growl at the bear.

"Look at Jip!" laughed Agatha. "He's acting like a ferocious lion." She picked up the bear and waggled it in front of Jip's face. "Grr!" she growled. "Come and get me, Jip!"

Jip leaped up and yanked the bear out of Agatha's hands, then scampered across the lawn, dragging the bear by its leg. "Jip!" called Samantha. "Stop!"

"Let's go get him!" yelled Agatha. Agnes knocked over her chair in her hurry to get up. All the girls squealed with glee. They jumped out of their chairs and ran after Jip and the twins.

Jip led the girls to the back of the house, in dizzy circles around the oak tree, across the drive, through the lilac hedge, and into the Rylands' yard. Finally, they caught up with him next to the Rylands' birdbath.

"Grab him!" yelled Agatha. She started to take a running leap.

"No, stop!" said Samantha. "I've got a better

18

idea." She took off her shoe and dangled it in front of Jip. "Here, Jip," she called in a friendly voice.

Jip perked up his ears. "Come and get the shoe, Jip," Samantha said. And sure enough, Jip dropped the teddy bear, trotted over to Samantha, and grabbed the shoe in his mouth. Samantha quickly picked him up. His paws left muddy polka dots on her lacy pinafore.

"Hurray!" cheered the girls.

"But where's the bear?" asked Edith Eddleton.

"I have it," someone said in a bragging voice. And there was Eddie, holding Samantha's teddy bear by its nose.

"Eddie Ryland, you give me that teddy bear," ordered Samantha.

"No!" said Eddie. "Not unless you let me play with that dog." He pointed at Jip. "And I want some ice cream, too. I helped make it."

"You can't play with Jip because he belongs to my Aunt Cornelia," Samantha said firmly. "And you can't have any ice cream because it's for my party."

"And *you* are not invited," said Agatha.

"Absolutely not," said Agnes. "This party

is only for girls."

"No boys are allowed," said Agatha. "Isn't that right, girls?"

Everyone chimed in, "Right! No boys are allowed."

"Then I'll keep the bear," said Eddie stubbornly.

"Eddie, you are a nincompoop!" said Agnes.

"Nincompoop!" said all the girls, laughing. It tickled their mouths to say such a funny word. "Eddie is a nincompoop! Eddie is a nincompoop!" they taunted. But before they could say nincompoop again, Agatha tackled Eddie around the knees and knocked him to the ground. She ripped the bear out of his hands and ran back through the hedge, with all the girls clapping and cheering behind her in a wild stampede.

The stampede stopped short at the circle of chairs. There stood Grandmary, waiting. "My heavens!" said Grandmary. "Whatever has happened?"

"Oh, Grandmary," panted Samantha. "Jip ran off with the teddy bear and we had to chase him." She didn't mention the part about tackling Eddie, since she *knew* that was breaking Grandmary's rule about fighting.

"I see," said Grandmary. "Well, I hope you weren't making a spectacle of yourselves." She looked around at the out-of-breath girls. Agnes' sash was untied. Agatha had grass stains on her stockings. Samantha's circlet of roses was tilted over one ear, like a halo gone wrong. Ida Dean had lost her hairbow entirely. Grandmary looked almost as if she might smile, but she didn't. Instead, she said, "You ladies seem to be a bit warm from your exercise. Perhaps this is the perfect time to have a cooling drink of lemonade."

Grandmary led the girls up the stairs of the porch to the birthday table. It was set with a beautiful lace cloth, Grandmary's best gold spoons, and a big crystal pitcher of pink lemonade. There was a little nosegay of pink roses at each place. After they sat down, Samantha gave each girl a favor—a lovely lace fan.

The girls tried to act like young ladies again, opening and closing their fans and fluttering them elegantly in front of their faces. They nibbled on

thin tea sandwiches and sipped daintily from their
goblets of lemonade. When Mrs. Hawkins carried
out the tray of ten tiny cakes all glowing with
candles, the girls gasped with delight. Everyone
sang "Happy Birthday" and clapped politely
when Samantha blew out all the candles in one
whoosh.

"This is such an elegant party," said Agnes as
Mrs. Hawkins put one of the petit fours on her
plate.

"Would you care for some ice cream?"
Samantha asked in her most grown-up voice as
Hawkins began serving.

"Oh! Molded ice cream!" chirped Ruth. "Just
like in a fancy ice cream parlor!"

"And wait till you taste it!" exclaimed Agnes.

All the girls put rather large, unladylike
spoonfuls in their mouths. Their faces turned as
pink as the ice cream.

"Ugh!"

"Eew!"

"Ick!"

"Awful!"

The girls coughed and choked. They spat the

ice cream out into their napkins. They slurped down gulps of lemonade. They clutched their throats and stuck out their tongues. They sputtered and gasped and gagged.

"SALT!" said Samantha. "This ice cream is full of salt!"

Hawkins looked puzzled. "But just a few minutes ago young Master Eddie tasted it, and he didn't complain."

"Was Eddie alone with the ice cream?" asked Samantha.

"Why, yes, I suppose he was," answered

Hawkins. "Just before I put it into the molds."

"That rotten Eddie!" exclaimed Agnes. "He put salt in the ice cream and ruined it for all of us!"

"Where is he? I'll fix him," threatened Agatha, frowning fiercely. She jumped up and ran smack into Cornelia.

"Whoa!" said Cornelia. "What's the matter, Agatha?" She looked around at the girls. "Why do you all look so sour?"

"Not sour," explained Samantha. "Salty. Eddie Ryland put salt in the ice cream and it's *ruined*."

Aunt Cornelia tasted the ice cream. "My stars!" she said. "You're right!" She looked at the disappointed girls. "Well," she said briskly, "you certainly can't eat *that*! But you still have lovely petit fours and delicious lemonade. Just ignore the ice cream."

All the girls carefully pushed the bowls of salty ice cream toward the center of the table. They ate their petit fours in silence. Samantha could hardly swallow, she felt so angry and sad. Her beautiful, elegant birthday party had been spoiled. But Agnes and Agatha finished eating quickly and hurried away from the table. They whispered with Cornelia for a few moments, then bounded back over to Samantha.

"We have the most wonderful idea!" crowed Agnes. "You're going to come to New York!"

"Ooooh!" sighed all the girls. "New York!"

"Cornelia says if it's all right with Grandmary, you can come to New York and stay at her new house," said Agatha.

"You can come next week," said Agnes. "We'll be there, too, and we can all go to Tyson's Ice Cream Parlor for the best ice cream in New York."

"With no Eddie Ryland to spoil it," said Agatha, the fierce gleam back in her eyes.

"I'd love that," said Samantha. The twins' latest idea made the disappointment of salty ice cream melt away. "May I go?" she asked Grandmary.

"Of course you may," said Grandmary. "And I shall go with you. I've been looking forward to peppermint ice cream myself!"

CHAPTER
THREE

—

NEW YORK CITY

New York City! Just the name was magic! Samantha leaned forward to peek out of the horse-drawn cab. She and Grandmary were riding along the busy city streets from the train station to Gard and Cornelia's new house. Samantha held on to her hat and twisted her head around, trying to see to the tops of the buildings. Everything in New York was so big! There were so many people hurrying along the sidewalks. In New York it always seemed as if something exciting was about to happen.

"I can't wait to see Agnes and Agatha," Samantha said to Grandmary.

"You do have a good time with them, don't

you, dear?" said Grandmary.

"They're always so much fun," said Samantha.

"They are happy, lively girls," agreed Grand-mary. "Though they do get a bit carried away with their ideas sometimes."

Samantha understood what Grandmary meant about Agnes and Agatha. Sometimes their ideas were as tangled as their bouncy red curls. "They're always thinking up new ways to do things," Samantha went on.

"Yes," said Grandmary. "But I'm afraid they don't always think very carefully. Besides, they don't realize that many times the old ways are still the best ways."

Suddenly, the cab jerked to a stop. Grandmary and Samantha leaned forward to look out. They were stopped at the edge of a big park. The sidewalk was so crowded, people spilled out into the street. Samantha saw some women hanging large banners across the entrance to the park. One banner said, "WOMEN FIGHT FOR YOUR RIGHT TO VOTE." Another banner said, "NOW IS THE TIME FOR CHANGE."

"We'll have to go another way, ma'am," the

cab driver called down to Grandmary. "These ladies seem to be blocking traffic all around Madison Square Park."

"Very well, do what you think is best," Grandmary answered. She sat back. She didn't seem to want to look at what was going on.

But Samantha was fascinated. "What's happening here?" she asked Grandmary.

"Well, it appears that a group of women are having a meeting in that park," Grandmary replied.

"Who are they?" Samantha asked.

"They're suffragettes," Grandmary answered. "They think women should be able to vote, so they get together and make a ruckus about changing the laws." She sat up very straight. "It's all just new-fangled notions."

The cab turned down a quieter street and Samantha sat back. She was still very curious about the meeting in the park, but she could tell by the look on Grandmary's face that she should not ask any more questions about it.

They rode in silence until the cab stopped in front of Gard and Cornelia's tall, narrow brownstone house.

Samantha had just hopped out onto the sidewalk when she heard voices shouting, "Samantha! Samantha!" She looked up. Agnes and Agatha were leaning out of a window high above her, waving wildly. Agnes held up Jip and waved his paw. Jip barked and wriggled with joy.

"Hello!" Samantha called. She skipped and waved, already swept away by the twins' high spirits.

"We'll be right down!" Agatha yelled. Then she and Agnes and Jip disappeared from the window.

Cornelia smiled as she came down the front steps to Samantha and Grandmary. "Welcome!" she said. Just then the twins and Jip came flying out the door and down the steps. "Hurray! You're here!" they said as they hugged Samantha. Aunt Cornelia laughed. "Come in, come in," she said. "As you can see, we're all very glad you're here."

The twins led Samantha into the dark, cool house. Uncle Gard was waiting just inside the doorway. He blinked at Samantha and said, "There you are, Sam! I've been looking for you all week long. I can't seem to find anything in this new house."

"Do you think you could help us find some lunch?" asked Aunt Cornelia.

"Certainly, certainly," said Uncle Gard, kissing the tip of her nose. "When it comes to finding food, I never have any trouble."

"Come on, Samantha!" said Agnes and Agatha. They pulled her into the dining room and made her sit between them. Then both at once they began showering her with questions. "Have you seen that terrible Eddie? How was your train ride? Do you want to go to the park after lunch? Do you want—"

"Girls!" Aunt Cornelia scolded gently as the maid began to pass the food. "You'll put Samantha in a spin with all your questions! There will be plenty of time for chatter later. I haven't even had a chance to ask Grandmary where she plans to shop today."

"I'll shop at O'Neill's, of course," replied Grandmary. "I never go any farther."

"There's a fine new shop on Fifth Avenue that's closer than O'Neill's," said Uncle Gard. "What was the name of that store, Cornelia?"

Grandmary patted his arm and smiled. "Don't trouble yourself to remember, Gardner," she said.

"I shall go to O'Neill's. I've shopped there for more than thirty years. I'm too old to change my ways now."

"O'Neill's is near Madison Square Park," said Aunt Cornelia slowly. "That area may be quite crowded today. There's a meeting in the park."

"I know," said Grandmary. "We passed it on our way from the station. Those suffragettes were already blocking traffic." She shook her head. "In my opinion, ladies should not gather in public places. *Especially* not to carry on about this voting nonsense."

"Nonsense?" Aunt Cornelia asked. Her voice rose ever so slightly.

"Of course," said Grandmary. "Voting is not a lady's concern. It never has been. I see no reason to change things now. Those suffragettes are making spectacles of themselves. They should stay at home where ladies belong."

Samantha saw Agnes and Agatha look at each other with raised eyebrows, then quickly look down into their soup bowls.

Aunt Cornelia opened her mouth to say

31

something, then shut it again.

Samantha was bursting with curiosity. "But why—" she began to ask.

"Well, well, well," interrupted Uncle Gard. "Well, well. The strangest thing happened to me as I was walking home from work the other day. A man came up to me and said, 'Do you know any girls who just turned ten years old?' And I said, 'Why, yes, in fact I do know one.' And he said, 'Would you give her this large box? There's something inside she might like.' So I brought the box home. It's out in the hall. Perhaps you'll open it, Sam, and show us what's inside."

Samantha forgot all about her questions. She and the twins ran from the table and opened the door. Jip was waiting right outside. He barked and jumped as the twins helped Samantha tear off the wrapping paper and open the box. Inside was a pram—the prettiest doll's carriage Samantha had ever seen. It was deep red with shiny brass wheels. "Jiminy!" Samantha whispered. "It's beautiful!" She ran to give Uncle Gard a big hug. "Thank you, Uncle Gard! Thank you very much!" She knew perfectly well the doll carriage was from Uncle Gard and no one else.

"Let's take it to the park right now!" suggested Agnes.

"That *would* be fun!" Samantha said eagerly. "May we go?"

"Certainly!" said Uncle Gard.

"Can Jip come, too?" asked Agatha. "You know how he loves the park."

"No, I don't think that is a good idea," said Aunt Cornelia. "Remember what happened at Samantha's party when he ran away from you?"

"Oh, but nothing like that will happen *here*," said Agatha quickly. "The park has a fence all around it."

"Please, please, please?" begged Agnes.

Aunt Cornelia thought for a moment.

"We'll only be across the street in the park," wheedled Agatha.

"And you won't go any farther than that?" asked Aunt Cornelia.

"No!" the twins promised together.

"Will you keep Jip on his leash?"

"Yes!" shouted the girls.

"Promise?"

"Absolutely!" they cried.

"Well, all right," Cornelia finally agreed. "But—"

"Hurray!" the twins interrupted. Jip began yipping in excitement.

"Please be calm for just a minute," Aunt Cornelia said seriously. "I'm going to a meeting, but I'll be back at three-thirty. When I get back, we'll walk to the ice cream parlor to meet Grandmary. Don't forget."

"And don't forget to behave like young ladies," added Grandmary.

"And don't forget the rule about keeping Jip on the leash," repeated Aunt Cornelia.

"And don't forget to have a good time," said Uncle Gard, shaking his finger at them.

"We won't!" said the girls. And Jip barked to show that he agreed.

FOLLOW THAT DOG!

Jip led a very cheerful parade to Gramercy Park. He pranced along the sidewalk, pulling at his leash. Agnes and Agatha skipped to keep up with him. Samantha followed behind, proudly pushing her new doll carriage. Even the doll Agnes had loaned her, which was rather tired-looking, seemed to perk up as she rode in the fine red pram out in the midday sunshine.

Gramercy Park was a pretty rectangular green across the street from Gard and Cornelia's house. It was fenced on all four sides by tall black iron railings with two locked gates. The buildings that surrounded it seemed to look down on the quiet little park fondly, as if they wanted to protect it from the hubbub of the city.

Agnes unlocked one gate and the girls followed Jip into the park. He zigzagged from one side of the path to the other, sniffing out interesting scents as he led the girls to a large fountain in the center of the park. Around the bottom of the fountain there was a pool where tin swans swam. "How pretty," said Samantha. "The swans look almost real."

Jip seemed to agree with Samantha. He growled at the swans and dragged on his leash, trying to get at them.

"Stop it, Jip," scolded Agatha, jerking him back. She tried to pull Jip away, but he lunged and leapt, barking wildly all the while. "Jip's pulling my arm out," complained Agatha.

"You'd better carry him," suggested Samantha.

So Agatha picked Jip up, but he kept barking even when they walked away from the fountain. When Agatha put him down, Jip tried to run back to the swans, so she had to pick him up again. He squirmed in her arms. "I'm tired of carrying Jip," Agatha whined. "You take him, Agnes."

"Absolutely not," said Agnes. "He'll get paw prints all over my dress. I don't want to be a mess like you are. After all," she said in a hoity-toity voice, "ladies do not make spectacles of themselves."

Samantha had to laugh. Agnes sounded just like Grandmary.

"Well, it's not fair," grumbled Agatha. "I've carried Jip enough. It was your dumb idea to bring him."

"It was not," said Agnes.

"It was too," said Agatha.

"It was not."

"It was too."

"Oh, *I'll* carry him," Samantha said firmly. "You push the pram, Agatha."

Agatha eyed the doll carriage. "No," she said. "I have a better idea."

"What now?" asked Agnes.

"Let's put Jip in the pram. That way none of us will have to carry him," said Agatha.

Agnes was instantly enthusiastic. "Oh, that *is* a good idea!" she said. "He can sit right next to the doll."

But Samantha didn't think it sounded like such a good idea. "We promised Cornelia we wouldn't let Jip off the leash," she reminded the twins.

"We're not going to let *Jip* off the leash," said Agatha. "We're going to let *me* off the leash. Just watch." Agatha slipped the leash off her wrist and put Jip in the pram. She looped the leash over the handle of the pram. "There! You see!" she said. "He's perfectly safe."

Samantha shook her head. "I don't think—"

Agnes interrupted, "Oh, don't be such a worrywart, Samantha. This is a brand new way to walk a dog. It's a great idea. Doesn't Jip look cute?"

And Jip did look cute, but only for one second. He yanked the leash with his mouth and pulled it off the handle. Then, before the girls could grab him, he leapt out of the carriage and took off like a streak.

"STOP!" shouted Samantha. "Jip, stop!" She started to run after him, trying to grab the leash dragging in the dirt.

"Jip! Jip! Jip! Jip! Jip!" Agatha yelped. She hopped up and down, waving her arms.

"Oh, no!" wailed all three girls when they saw Jip wiggle between the iron bars of the fence and slip out of the park. Just for a second, he turned to look at them.

"What'll we do now?" groaned Agnes. "Cornelia will be furious!"

"Quick! Climb over the fence!" yelled Agatha wildly. She ran to the fence and started to shinny up the iron bars. "Split up! Get the firemen! Call the police!"

Agnes just stood still, holding her face in her hands, moaning.

Samantha saw that she was going to have to take charge. "Don't just stand there!" she ordered. "We've got to catch him! Come on!" She led the twins to the gate and pushed it open. They could see Jip halfway down the block, his white tail waving like a feather as he trotted along. The gate swung shut behind them.

"Your doll carriage!" cried Agnes.

"Leave it," Samantha said as she ran. "We've *got* to get Jip!"

The three girls took off after Jip. He was running toward a big hotel on the corner. Samantha

As the girls dashed after Jip,
Samantha heard a frightening rumble overhead.

41

saw a group of people waiting in front with piles of luggage around them. "Stop that dog!" she called. But Jip was too fast. He bounded through the crowd, jumped over a trunk, and slipped around the corner.

As the girls dashed after him, Samantha heard a frightening rumble. A shower of soot fell like black snow. She looked up for one second to see a train running along a track built up over the street. When she looked down again, Jip had disappeared.

"Where'd he go?" she gasped to Agnes.

"I don't know," Agnes wailed. "We've lost him. Forever and ever!"

"Not if I can help it!" said Samantha. She ran up to a man pushing a cart full of strawberries. "Have you seen our dog?" she asked urgently.

"Yes, yes!" said the man. "He went that way." He pointed farther up the street.

"Thanks!" yelled Samantha.

"There he is!" shouted Agatha. They saw Jip's tail bouncing along ahead of a wagon overflowing with flowers. The wagon looked just like Grandmary's garden in Mount Bedford. But chasing Jip in New York City was a lot different from chasing him in Mount Bedford. The city was so big, and Jip was so little. What if they lost him? What if—

CLANG! CLANG! CLANG!

Samantha practically jumped out of her skin as a big streetcar rumbled up to the curb in front of her. The huge sweaty horses that pulled it shook their harnesses, snorting as they waited for people to get off. Samantha looked at the heavy hooves and thought how easily Jip could be crushed by them.

"Now where is he?" cried Agnes.

"I see him," said Agatha. "On the other side of the street."

The girls dashed across the street, weaving between a wagon full of rattling milk cans and an automobile whose horn blared at them. Jip was far ahead of them now, slithering like a snake through the crowd. It was hard for the girls to move very fast because the sidewalk was so full of people. They had to wiggle their way between fashionable ladies, gentlemen in straw hats, boys selling newspapers, and workmen carrying heavy loads.

"'Scuse me, 'scuse me," said Samantha as she and

the twins jostled past the people.

Agatha tripped over a loose brick in the sidewalk and fell to her knees. "Ow!" she wailed, almost in tears. She knelt on the sidewalk. "Go ahead, leave me behind."

"No," said Samantha. She helped Agatha get up and dusted her off. "You're fine. Come on," she said. "You can't stop now. We need you. You're the best one at spotting Jip."

None of them saw Jip again until they got to the corner of Fifth Avenue, the widest and busiest street in New York. "Look!" called Agatha, pointing with both hands. "There's Jip! In the street!"

Samantha leapt off the curb to get him when suddenly the pavement shook beneath her feet. Someone yanked her back up onto the sidewalk. She was almost crushed in the tumble of people who scrambled to get back on the curb. "Watch out!" a voice shouted. "Fire engine! Out of the way!"

"JIP!" yelled Samantha. She caught a glimpse of Jip, but then two huge horses galloped in front of her, pulling a fire engine. Its deafening bell rang out over the shouts and screams from the crowd.

The firemen clung to the shiny pump in the middle
of the wagon as it stormed past in a blur of red
and silver, stirring up a cloud of dust in the street,
racing like the wind.

"Jip," Samantha whispered. Was Jip somewhere
in that cloud of dust? Nothing moved in the street.
"Oh, Jip, we never should have let you go."

CHANGES

The fire engine roared off around the corner. The dust settled. Samantha stood on the curb, gathering her courage to go out into the street and look for Jip.

Agnes and Agatha ran up to her. "Where is he?" Agnes asked breathlessly. "Where's Jip? Do you see him?"

Samantha shook her head no. "I think he might . . . he might be . . ."

"There he is!" shouted Agatha, hopping up and down. "Look! He's going into that park across the street."

"I see him!" shouted Samantha. She was so relieved. "Come on! Now we've *got* to catch him."

The girls dashed across the street into the park. Jip trip-trotted ahead of them as if he knew exactly where he was going and nothing would stop him. He darted through a crowd of women who were all headed toward a platform draped with signs and flags.

"Oh, no!" Agnes gulped. "This is Madison Square Park! Where the suffragettes' meeting is!"

"Quick! Let's get out of here!" said Agatha in a panic.

"No," said Samantha. "We've got to get Jip. Grandmary won't mind if we're in the park for just a minute to get the dog."

"It's not Grandmary we're worried about," interrupted Agnes. "It's Cornelia. She's here. And if she sees us, she'll be furious. She thinks we're back in Gramercy Park."

"Cornelia?" Samantha gasped. "What's *she* doing here?"

"She's at the meeting about women voting," Agatha said quickly. "We heard her tell Gard she was coming. He said Grandmary wouldn't like it. But Cornelia said she could think for herself and she was coming anyway."

Samantha was very confused. What was Cornelia doing with the suffragettes? Grandmary said these women were making spectacles of themselves. Was Cornelia doing something wrong? But Samantha didn't have time to think. Agnes grabbed her arm. "Come on!" she ordered. "Let's get Jip and *go.*"

The girls chased Jip to a small pool with a fountain in the middle. He eyed the girls. As they came closer, he edged away. "Give him some room," said Samantha. "We don't want him to—"

SPLASH! Jip jumped into the pool!

"I'll dive in and get him!" Agatha cried. She pulled off her shoe.

"WAIT!" said Samantha quickly. She grabbed Agatha's shoe and waved it in front of Jip, just as she had in Mount Bedford. "Look, Jip!" she said in a friendly voice. "A shoe. Come and get it."

Jip looked at the shoe. He began to paddle across the pool toward Samantha. Just then, the crowd got very quiet. "Ladies and gentlemen," a woman's voice began.

Jip stopped. He tilted his head and perked up his ears. When the speaker said, "Welcome!" Jip yelped with joy. He sprang out of the pool, splattering water all over the girls. Before they could grab him, he scampered up the steps of the speakers' platform, yipping and yapping wildly. He ran right up to the woman who was standing in front of everyone.

"CORNELIA!" gasped all three girls. The speaker was Cornelia! Jip wiggled from head to tail, sending a spray of water all over her.

"Jip? What are you doing here?" Cornelia asked. Jip barked excitedly, and she scooped him up in her arms. "Well," she said, turning to the crowd, "this eager fellow wants to speak, too!"

The crowd clapped and laughed.

Cornelia's voice was strong and firm as she went on. "The time has come for all of us to speak out. We must stand up for what we believe is right!" she said. "We must make up our own minds. The time has come to change the old ways. Women *must* vote!"

The crowd clapped louder than ever. Some women waved banners and cheered. Cornelia carried Jip back to her seat and another woman rose

49

"CORNELIA!" gasped all three girls.
The speaker was Cornelia!

to speak. As Cornelia sat down, she looked all around, searching for faces in the crowd.

"Jeepers! She's looking for us!" whispered Agnes.

"Well, she's got Jip, so let's get out of here!" said Agatha.

"No," said Samantha. "We can't do that. We have to face her and admit what we did."

The twins looked at each other uncomfortably.

"Maybe you're right," sighed Agatha.

The girls waited nervously while other suffragettes spoke. When all the speeches were over and the crowd had begun to wander away, Cornelia came down from the platform. She walked toward the girls. "Well," she said without a trace of her usual smile. "What are *you*—and Jip—doing here?"

The girls looked down at their shoes. "We did a very stupid thing," Samantha began.

"It was really a terrible idea," admitted Agnes.

"We put Jip in the pram," said Samantha. "And we didn't hold on to the leash, so he ran away."

Agatha burst out, "But we didn't think he'd—"

51

"You certainly *didn't* think," Cornelia cut in. "You just went right ahead with your own ideas and didn't pay any attention to what I said about keeping Jip on the leash. That was an important rule and one we all agreed on. When will you girls learn that you can't just change things when you feel like it?"

"But aren't you trying to change things?" asked Agatha. "Aren't you trying to get women to vote?"

"That's very different, Agatha," answered Cornelia. "All the women here today have thought long and hard about changing the laws so that women can vote. When you want to change something, you'd better be sure it's a wise change, a change for the better."

The girls were silent. Finally Samantha said, "We're very sorry, Aunt Cornelia. We really are."

Cornelia shook her head. "I believe you are sorry," she said. "You certainly look sorry. In fact, you look like a sorry mess." Her voice had a little laugh in it. She looked at her watch. "Oh, my gracious! It's nearly three-thirty. We'll be late meeting Grandmary if we don't leave right now. There's no time to go home and change. We'll have to go to Tyson's as untidy as we are."

The girls were rumpled and wrinkled and Cornelia's dress was covered with muddy paw prints, so it was a very bedraggled parade that Jip led to the ice cream parlor. When they got to Tyson's, Samantha saw Grandmary sitting at a corner table near the gleaming soda fountain. Her face was rather red, and Samantha was afraid she might be angry.

Samantha rushed ahead of Cornelia and the twins. "Grandmary," she blurted out, "we're sorry to be so late and sorry that we look so messy, but we've had the most awful time. Agnes and Agatha and I nearly lost Jip. We chased him everywhere, and finally he ran into Madison Square Park. Remember, the place where the cab stopped this morning? Jip jumped into a fountain there, and just when we almost caught him, he got away again. But it was all right because he ran onto the speakers' platform and right up to—" Samantha stopped. "Oh, no," she said. She didn't want to tell Grandmary about Cornelia.

But Cornelia finished for Samantha. "Jip ran

*"Grandmary," Samantha blurted out, "we're sorry to be so late
and sorry that we look so messy, but we've had the most awful time."*

54

right up to *me*," she said, looking Grandmary straight in the eye. "*I* was on the speakers' platform."

"I know you were on the platform," said Grandmary. "I saw you. I was at the meeting myself."

"You were?" everyone gasped.

"Yes," said Grandmary firmly. "I was on my way here to Tyson's. But there were so many people around the park that I couldn't get by. When I saw *you* up on the platform, Cornelia, I thought perhaps I ought to stay and listen." Grandmary took Cornelia's hand. "My dear," she said, "I must admit that what I saw and what I heard gave me a bit of a surprise. I've always said that I'm too old to change my ways, but I've changed my mind today."

Grandmary touched her forehead with her handkerchief. Samantha saw that her hat was tipped back a little, as if she'd turned around very suddenly. "You and the other ladies who spoke today were simply saying that women should stand up for what they think is right. That's exactly what I believe, too. And if that's what voting will give us a chance to do, then I think women *should* vote. The time for change *has* come."

Cornelia smiled at Grandmary. "Yes, it is time to change the old rules," she said. "And that's what makes this a wonderful time for these young ladies to be growing up."

"Well, growing up is what we've come to celebrate, isn't it?" asked Grandmary. "Shall we have our ice cream?"

She turned to Samantha. "Peppermint for you, my dear? Or would you like to try something new today?"

"No, thank you," smiled Samantha. "Peppermint is my old favorite. There are some things that are just too good to change."

LOOKING
BACK
1904

A Peek Into
the Past

Nursemaids took care of babies.

At the turn of the century, when girls like Samantha were growing up, babies were born at home. Usually a doctor was there to help the mother, while the father and other family members waited in another room. The birth of a new baby was a very special event, and the newest member of a family was quite pampered. If parents could afford to, they hired a nursemaid or nanny who would bathe, dress, feed, and entertain the baby. Nursemaids dressed babies in fancy long dresses and ruffled bonnets. They took them for walks in elaborate carriages called *prams*. A baby usually had its own special room called the *nursery*.

By the time a child started to walk,

Elegant prams had umbrellas.

58

Young children had tea in their nursery.

the nursery became a playroom and a dining room as well as a bedroom. Children ate most of their meals in the nursery instead of in the dining room with their parents. They sat at child-sized tables and chairs and used child-sized dishes. They kept their toys and books in the nursery and played with them there.

Before the turn of the century, most American children did not have a lot of time to play. Instead, they were expected to help their parents with farming and housework. By the time children like Samantha were growing up, adults wanted children to play. They understood that childhood was a

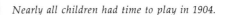
Nearly all children had time to play in 1904.

59

Illustrations from books in 1904

special stage of life. They built city parks with playgrounds for children. They invented new toys and games that were sold in toy stores and catalogues. And they passed laws that said children were not allowed to work in factories so that all boys and girls could have time to play.

When children like Samantha played, they sometimes pretended to be doing grown-up jobs. Girls used miniature stoves, sewing machines, and carpet sweepers to pretend they were keeping house. They also pretended that they were mothers, using dolls that looked like babies or small children.

Toy stove and sewing machine

Girls and boys enjoyed reading books like *Alice in Wonderland* and *The Wizard of Oz.* Teddy bears were a popular new toy in 1904. Games like checkers and dominoes were popular, too.

At the turn of the century, clothing styles made children look very different from grownups. But often

The barefoot child in this picture is a boy!

boys and girls didn't look very different from one another! Many boys wore their hair in long curls, and both young girls and young boys wore dresses. As boys grew older, they dressed in short pants or *breeches*, and then in long trousers. It was never considered proper for girls to wear long pants or shorts.

Even though children were expected to play and have fun at the turn of the century, adults wanted them to grow up to be ladies and gentlemen. By the time girls were eight or nine they went to dancing school, took music lessons, learned to paint, and did fancy sewing. They were allowed to join the adults for meals in the dining room. And they practiced grown-up manners and conversation when they went to birthday parties or went *calling* on friends with their mothers.

By the time Samantha and her friends were fifteen, they looked and

Calling cards and dancing school were part of growing up.

Corset, curling iron, and hairpins

acted more like adults than like young children. They wore long dresses in adult styles that made them look grown-up. Instead of wearing huge hairbows and long curls, they used pins and combs to put their hair up in elegant styles. They began wearing corsets to keep their figures looking trim.

Many of them stopped going to school or went to a *finishing school* where they finished their education as proper young ladies. At a finishing school they learned how to manage servants, how to run an orderly household, and how to give parties.

Once they turned eighteen, girls like Samantha became part of the grown-up world. Some had *coming out* or *debutante* parties, which introduced them to elegant society. Others followed different paths and went to college or got jobs. Some became suffragettes and worked for women's votes. From that time on, whatever young ladies chose to do, they left childhood behind forever.

Some girls became debutantes. Some became suffragettes.

THE AMERICAN GIRLS COLLECTION®

FELICITY   KIRSTEN®   ADDY   SAMANTHA   MOLLY

There are more books in The American Girls Collection. They're filled with the adventures that five lively American girls lived long ago.

The books are the heart of The American Girls Collection, but they are only the beginning. There are also lovable dolls that have beautiful clothes and lots of wonderful accessories. They make these stories of the past come alive today for American girls like you.

To learn about The American Girls Collection, fill out this postcard and mail it to Pleasant Company, or call **1-800-845-0005.** We will send you a catalogue about all the books, dolls, dresses, and other delights in The American Girls Collection.

I'm an American girl who loves to get mail. Please send me a catalogue of The American Girls Collection®:

My name is _____

My address is _____

City_____ State _____ Zip_____

Parent's signature _____

And send a catalogue to my friend:

My friend's name is _____

Address _____

City_____ State _____ Zip_____

The book this postcard is in came from:
☐ a bookstore   ☐ a library   ☐ a friend/relative   ☐ Pleasant Company's Catalogue

If the postcard has already been removed from this book and you would like to receive a Pleasant Company catalogue, please send your name and address to:

PLEASANT COMPANY
P.O. Box 620497
Middleton, WI 53562-9940
or, call our toll-free number
1-800-845-0005